Last Bench

Poems for Teens

N. Periyasamy

Translated in English

By

Malarvizhi

Last Bench Poems for Teens
N. Periyasamy (Tamil)
Translation in English: Malarvizhi
Young Adult Literature
First Published: february, 2023

ONGIL KUTTAM &
BOOKS FOR CHILDREN - imprint of Bharathi Puthakalayam
7, Elango Salai, Teynampet, Chennai - 600 018
Email: bharathiputhakalayam@gmail.com | www.thamizhbooks.com
044 24332424,   24332924, 24356935

Design by : R. Kalathi

நினைத்த நூல்கள்... நினைத்த நேரத்தில்...   9498062424

Translator's note

Anna Ruscani said "Words travel worlds and the translator does the driving".

Translating is picking the best for the other world.

"Last Bench" is a collection of poems depicting the emotions and beliefs of the teen age students.

I enjoyed translating each poem. The idea behind these poems will definitely help them with their transition to adulthood.

This is a joyful start of my translation journey. Thanks to Periyasamy and Oongil kootam for providing me an opportunity to do the translation of this wonderful book portraying the feelings of a child's transition to adulthood. My heartfelt thanks to my family and friends for all the love and support.

Foreword

N.Periyasamy is one of the well-known poets in Tamilnadu. He is fondly called as "Perusu" by his friends. He is a person with smiling face and qualities like simplicity, easily approachable, good mannerism and who loosens easily for micro emotions. He is a fast reader of whatever books he receives. That too his norm is to celebrate the creation and creator. So, he has earned the love and friendship of many creators across Tamilnadu. We will wonder with his one book "Mozhiyin Nizhal", how he has introduced a vast range of books. His interest for poetry is exhibited clearly in the articles and we can easily experience the same. Next to poetry and articles, he has introduced the other forms of creative writing too in his book. Most of these tend to finish from one and half pages to maximum five pages.

Other than exhibiting deep human emotions for poetry collections, the way he uses modern poetry to describe the same is appreciable. We can see Periyasamy's deep involvement in the inner world of children in his poetry book "Kutty meengal nelinthodum aagayam". The rare ability of identifying the childhood in kids who place the ears on the floor and lisen to the murmers of the lake and pond inhabitants that has been buried long back under their house and worry about the same to their father and recording them as poems is found in very less people like Periyasamy. Roaming around with the children who paint what they observe with crayons and the unique ability to find their Sky with the little stars swimming around in a poetic way is a gifted uniqueness of Periyasamy.

When the poetry collection "Last Bench" was released, many have written articles appreciating the same, including me. Malar being a poet who read and enjoyed them, have translated them into English poems with the title "Last Bench" and has given it to the readers. The most legendary creations which has carried its fame over million years in Tamil are being translated to English in the recent times.

Last bench and the students who are forced to sit there are been avoided, as that is a punishment area. In the school classes, that is like the "No water forest". But since this collection has arrived it has shined and traversed from last bench to the first bench. The English and Tamil books that has been jointly published by Bharathi puthakalayam and Ongil Koottam has been received well and read by the readers.

In this book, we can experience the English translation is fluent and to the point. The mother who was rigid when the kids asked wanting to play running around or pleaded for the mobile "I will return after watching for five minutes" has lied "Your eyes will be spoiled and the brain will be affected". But locked up inside the house, the parents have forced the mobile phone to the kids, and made them sit for online classes. But the son was waiting for his freedom like a Swan. "I am waiting like a swan for a dawn so gold to free myself from the parents" says the English translation. The poem that celebrates sea as a wonder also says the boy's eyes that resembles the sunflower which drags the Sun rays towards it, was hopeless for one or two days and the conversation begins like this "His eyes filled with rain... The class teacher compares me with someone for everything. My talent is mine, right?". The last line in the English poem slaps on the face. It is the translation of "My talent is mine,Right?" still the depth of English language is powerful. The students pleading voice in the lines "Nowadays, I am praying to God often, to open the closed schools at least for the Corona to end" melts our heart.

He is not bothered about the last bench instead the only sorrow is not able to peep outside. In English this is the line of the last bench" Though he doesn't feel sad for the last bench, being unable to peep out is still a sadness". "Thothangoli" is a word used only in Tamilnadu that too specifically in certain districts local slang and I was eagerly waiting how Malar will translate it in English.

The simple word "Loser" is been placed. This is a simple word, but the fact is languages differ. "Ninaivu" poem is a tragic painting. "He gave the flowers he carried to the waves..He observed the floating flowers without a blink whose eyesight was blocked with tears.." when we keep both the Tamil and English poems next to each other and read them, the pain strikes double.

Oongil Koottam has already translated Vishnupuram Saravanan's "Kayiru" story and released the same. It got an exciting reception and now Last bench. This has to be continued.

With wishes,
Kamalalayan

1

Fake nest

"Just 5 minutes mom

Will give it back soon" I plead

"You will lose your eyesight

and it affects your thoughts" you denied

all these reasons were lies!!

When I roam around

or play in ground

and deny to come...

you give me a phone

and make me sit for the sessions online

I am waiting like a swan for a dawn so gold

to free myself from the parents hold.

2

Sea the wonder

The different types of fishes that scatter

with colours that glitter

The wave that swirls and plays

by making its own body with salt

the magic that opens and closes

It is the crabs that roam on the land

that makes us happy

Within the time of an eye blink

It took us like a mother lap

to save human lives

who worship it as a God

let us celebrate it without

littering the shore.

3

Joyful dance

He was bouncing

back and forth like a ball

here and there

He grabbed his mother's mobile

and caught videos on a roll

He invited his neighbour

and showed them

the bird that sat in the tree

in front of his home

was the one that came in his dream

He uploaded the video on his channel

The next day danced joyfully

for the thousand likes he received!!

4

Allergic

I initiated the conversation with a person

whose face reminds us

of the Yellow sunflower

that attracts the sun rays

who was upset last 2 days

And as he longed for it

His eyes filled with rain

he said

"The class teacher compares me with someone for everything"

I feel allergic

my talent is mine, right ?

5

Generation

" Do you know what my classmate Kishore did today?

he was repeating whatever the teacher said

and she left the class with anger..."

Said, my daughter...

At the same time

when I enjoyed my daughter's taste

I heard a yell

"Anytime, she speaks only about boys,

Ask her to be modest"

Said, her mom.

6

Dear Vahini

" I feel like saying this to you

with the changes in my body,

my affection is also increasing .

It feels bad to touch and talk

I came to know about the frequent touches

and learnt to avoid it

so you also be cautious"

- from the time I saw my girl friend's email

 I can feel a spider knitting a web inside me

and determined to identify the love

 that comes on its own, in my way.

7

Separated from class

The girl in the class who jumps like a calf

and burst like a mustard

was seen so tired and dull ...

The teacher had a secret conversation with her,

found what she didn't bring

and gave a handbag filled with motherness

Finally the napkin gave her that bloom back!!

8

Secret lie

Unusual like any day

"Mom, Mom" pampered the daughter

when she asked, what is your appeal for?

daughter replied "Today is Praveen's birthday

and he has invited us to his home.

I will be late in the evening".

She said "Okay, Okay

without forgetting, mention to father

that you went to a girl's home"

9

Freedom

Dear Priya,

Its been so many days I saw you

the video calls doesn't bring the happiness

of touch and feel

They are not letting me out of home

The time passes with the cat in the house

only my brothers are roaming out

and when I ask about it

They say "They are boys".

Nowadays I pray to god

corona has to end soon

at least to open the schools!!

10

Corona torture

The hands that hold the chalk

that reminds the baby holding the rattle

The curled hair string in the forehead

that reminds the question mark

The eyes that flutter like a butterfly

The saree worn perfectly

The sound of bangles that melt us like music

With all of these, we are longing to see the maths teacher

who solve the complex problems in a simple way.

11

Let us be teachers

This is the peepal tree

That is a squirrel tail

That is the aerial root of the banyan tree

see there is a butterfly

listen to the sounds of Cuckoo

see the hop of the babbler

Woodpecker that makes us to drum

group of parrots that fly when we tap

touch me not plant that shrinks on a touch

group of crows that are known for the disturbance

Let us remember

the teachers who taught us everything

from the beauty of the nature

with the lessons to be written as a story, maths,

song and dance

and let us turn ourselves as teachers too.

12

Tears that washed the mistakes

Like the old leaf, that was ready to fall on a touch

his eyes were filled with tears

After the class was over,

teacher took him to his room

Like longing to speak out, he started crying

before the teacher asked for the reason

as the teacher calmed him by twirling his hair

he cried "I made my father ashamed in front of every one"

Wiping his eyes he added "The police bet my father for
driving the bike fast" and cried

"Your tears has washed away your mistake,

don't panic" the teacher told and hugged him.

13

Murugan and Valli

Valli prayed to Lord Murugan

who was waiting behind the closed door

Tomorrow the school reopens

I will sit on my place where a heart stuck

with arrow is drawn

The Boy who frequently blinks his eyes named kanthan will
sit opposite to me

 I am going to see the grandmother

Who sells snacks in the school entrance

 I wish to kiss the Eshwari grandmother

who loves me so much

and sells jujube fruit, prickly pear cactus fruit and black night
shade fruit

None of the grandmother

should have died out of Corona

I prayed to break a coconut and do wetting

once the temples are open

send them safe God Muruga.

14

Last Bench

After completing the lesson, the teacher

asked the students a question

he replied "Squirrel is there"

Out of anger,

Teacher told to him to go to last bench

he is an expert in pulling the tender palm

in five minutes

from a fifty feet palm tree

he dives inside the deep well

 and brings the fallen buckets

and gets all the kisses

though he doesn't feel sad for the last bench

being unable to be peep out is

still a sadness!!

15

Jealous

When my friend said

"He has more value among the girls and

for each and everything all the teachers are praising him as he gets more marks in maths

no one value us..

let us see how he gets marks this time!!"

 I asked with surprise how that will happen?

he laughed and said " I stole his maths book yesterday itself".

16
Loser

On seeing the floating dragonflies in air

The boys wooped..

one of them announced the competition

each one should catch one and

which dragon fly carries more weight will win

those who accepted, ran for capturing them

only two captured the dragonflies, they made them   to carry the stones

the one who saw the mix of colours glitter in its eyes

allowed it to fly

They teased "You are the loser" and laughed at him.

17
Chlorine water

On top of the Motor room was one

on the branch of the tree was the other

One more was singing in the steps

the well opened its mouth and received those

who jumped like falling of a coconut branch

On a count of fifty, seventy and hundred

they played

by holding the breath under the water

Didn't you jump" the voice broke the memory

Reminded of the well

he jumped into the chlorinated pool water.

18

Letter

Dear Hrithik,

In the era of seeing in person and talking, what is the need for the letter

I too had this question...

The writer who came as chief guest for my school told stories about writing letter with happiness, sorrow, tears, we didn't know how the time went.

That moment a wish bloomed and I went to the post office.

 Distinct people and different wishes came alive there.

Rather than seeing in person and talking, writing a letter felt close.

I had visions about the feelings for you

and an untold feeling is withstanding inside my body.

you also write a letter and you too will definitely experience it.

Love,

Kishore

19

Taste of Notice

Driver uncle didn't you switch on the AC?

He said it's on repair and he lowered the window glass

as they crossed the flower shop

he disappeared in the fragrance in the air

moving certain distance the flavours of masala aroused the
hunger in his mind

He admired the beauty of Beatle leaves

rightly ordered like bunches of Banana

he wondered watching the old lady who sat behind the heap
of vegetables

it is the same path he travels everyday

rather than playing in mobile

For the first time

he enjoyed the taste of notice.

20

Question worm

When the Vijay TV serial got over and they were about to sleep

he said father, I have a doubt "How much is the education fees for a year?"

The father replied including admission, special class, yoga,Van fees

it will cross a lakh

The fees is more for now and

for college it will be still more

for that reason, we ask you to study well

So we will get a seat in Government Medical College

Father, for that we can join government school right now, isn't it?

father replies "Be calm and study

you will not understand"

"Government college is needed

government job is needed

why government school is not needed?"

There remained a question worm

Like a Beetle inside a Mango seed.

21

Joker

On the school annual day

With mixed colours of rainbow

the Joker appeared .

Auditorium indulged in joy

With or without talking

he made them laugh

"Look at the funny fellow" he said

And arbitrarily on seeing

his sister's laugh like never before

He realised the truth, that

making others laugh is

not just an act but

it's a wonderful art

After understanding it

for the first time

he saw the joker with respect now.

22

Swing

On seeing the mango pieces stacked in order,

it was mouth watering to see them

and entered the park

We got excited with the sound of the children

and our eyes searched for the swing

After the girls on the swing got down and left,

we enjoyed the swing happily

And on seeing a friend posing for a selfie

we wondered

how the sky also moved to and from with us.

23

Memory

He gave the flowers

he carried to the wave

He observed the floating flowers without a blink

Whose eye sight was blocked with tears

The day they both played by dabbing sand on each other

He dived in the wave and swam inside

"Enough...come back!!" we screamed

But unaware of that

The wave took him away.

"Carelessness kills a person"

repeats the guy in my dream

whose Memorial day is today.

24
Message

He forgot hunger

He reduced speaking

Remained unbathed

With unchanged dress

he stayed in the same place

considering it as the world

without a blink

he deleted

the other WhatsApp messages

As he was waiting

for the message from the girl he loves.

25

Celebration

The seats of the vehicles

turned to be the tables at the Midnight

To set the cake

and fill cool drinks it was 11:59 pm

The seconds hand of the clock

turned to be minutes hands

and went slow

At 12:00 am, they shouted "Ho:

the wishes filled cake was applied

on the birthday boy's face

the moon tasted it and the stars too!!

Author: N. Periyasamy

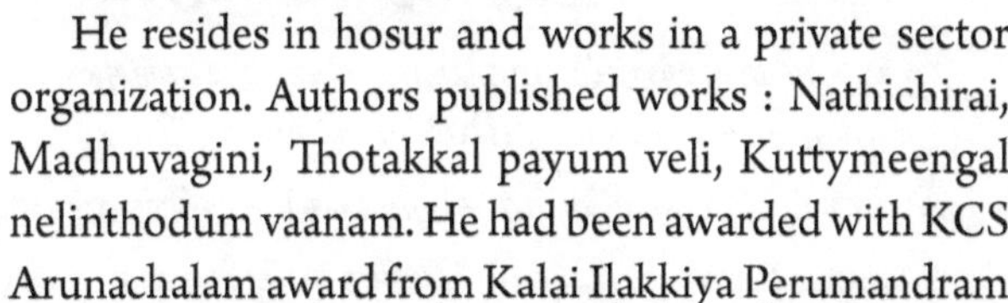

He resides in hosur and works in a private sector organization. Authors published works : Nathichirai, Madhuvagini, Thotakkal payum veli, Kuttymeengal nelinthodum vaanam. He had been awarded with KCS Arunachalam award from Kalai Ilakkiya Perumandram and Ashokamithran creative award. Mozhiyin Nizhal was his first essay collection book.

Translator: Malarvizhi

Malarvizhi is a budding writer with her native as coimbatore. She was formerly working as Technology Lead in IT and now she is pursuing her passion in literature. Her debut poetry book "Vidamal Thurathum Kadhal" was published in 2021. Foreword for her book was penned down by Kaviperarasu Vairamuthu. Her second poetry book "Judas maram" was released on December 2022. She is currently working on translation projects.

Oongil Kootam

Ongil Kootam: There has long been a demand for the publication of age-appropriate works in children's literature. Efforts to that end have been ongoing from time to time. 'Ongil Koottam' is a continuation of these efforts. Ongil Kootam continues to publish books for teenagers through collaborations with friends with a shared ideology. Ongil Kootam brings out booklets on different topics such as science, society, ecology, biographies of personalities to encourage children's reading habits. Ongil kootam's efforts in publishing books with beautiful illustrations in two languages, Tamil and English, in a simple language style, has been welcomed. Under the supervision of 'Kamalalayan', and coordination of 'Panchu Mittai' Prabhu, Ongil kootam continues its journey with the support of a group of writers, painters and designers.

Contact: editor.oongilkootam@gmail.com
Releases: https://amzn.to/3vfOvqX

Oongil Kootam books are available on print also (in collaboration with Bharathi Puthagalayam) : https://thamizhbooks.com/product/elaiyore-elakkiyam-set/

<h1 style="text-align:center">நமது பிற வெளியீடுகள்</h1>

1. மகர்கள் மற்றும் மாங்கர்களின் துயரங்கள் -
   முக்தா சால்வே, தமிழில்: திவ்யா பிரபு

2. கயிறு (இளையோர் சிறுகதை) - விஷ்ணுபுரம் சரவணன்

3. ஹம்போல்ட்: அவர் நேசித்த இயற்கை - ஹேமபிரபா

4. வாசிக்காத புத்தகத்தின் வாசனை - கொ.மா.கோ.இளங்கோ

5. சாலிம் அலி: உயரப் பறந்த இந்தியக் குருவி -
   ஆதி வள்ளியப்பன்

6. தண்ணீர் என்றோர் அமுதம் -
   சி.வி.ராமன், தமிழில்: கமலாலயன்

7. ஓரிகாமி (காகித மடிப்புக் கலையின் கதை) - தியாக சேகர்

8. சோசோவின் விசித்திர வாழ்க்கை - உதயசங்கர்

9. சார்லஸ் டார்வின்: கடல் பயணங்களால் உருவெடுத்த
   மேதை - அன்பு வாகினி

10. கடைசி பெஞ்ச் (இளையோருக்கான கவிதைகள்) -
    ந.பெரியசாமி

11. ஜானகி அம்மாள்: இந்தியாவின் கரும்புப் பெண்மணி
    - இ.பா. சிந்தன்

12. சாக்லேட்டி (இளையோருக்கான கவிதைகள்) -
    ராஜேஸ் கனகராஜன்

13. தோபா தேக் சிங் - சதத் ஹசன் மண்ட்டோ,
    தமிழில்: உதயசங்கர்

14. *Humboldt: A Scientist's encounter with nature (English)*
    - Hemaprabha, Translator: Ilamparithi

15. *Salim Ali (English) - Aadhi Valliappan,*
    Translator: Ilamparithi

16. *Kayiru - Vishnupuram Saravanan, Translator: Ilamparithi*

17. பகத் சிங் – ஏன் நாத்திகர் ஆனார் - சிவ சுப்ரமணியம்

18. *Last Bench - N.Periyasamy, Translator: Malarvizhi*

19. ஆழ்கடல்: சூழலும் வாழிடங்களும் -
    நாராயணி சுப்பிரமணியன்

20. சுல்தானாவின் கனவு - ரொக்கேயா பேகம்,
    தமிழில்: திவ்யா பிரபு

www.ingramcontent.com/pod-product-compliance
Lightning Source LLC
LaVergne TN
LVHW041809190726
843493LV00009B/2846